S0-AAZ-359

Are You My Mother?

Written and Illustrated by
P. D. EASTMAN

BEGINNER BOOKS

A Division of Random House, Inc.

To My Mother

All rights reserved.
Published in the United States by Random House Children's Books,
a division of Random House, Inc., New York.
Originally published by Random House Children's Books,
a division of Random House, Inc., New York, in 1960.

Beginner Books, Random House, and the Random House colophon
are registered trademarks of Random House, Inc.
The Cat in the Hat logo ® and © Dr. Seuss Enterprises, L.P. 1957,
renewed 1986. All rights reserved.

Visit us on the Web! www.randomhouse.com/kids

Educators and librarians, for a variety of teaching tools, visit us at
www.randomhouse.com/teachers

This title was originally cataloged by the Library of Congress as follows:
Eastman, Philip D.
Are you my mother? Written and illustrated by P. D. Eastman.
[New York] Beginner Books; distributed by Random House [1960]
63 p. illus. 24 cm.
(Beginner books B-18)
I. Title. PZ10.3.E1095Ar 60-13495
ISBN: 978-0-394-80018-9 (trade) ; ISBN: 978-0-394-90018-6 (lib. bdg.)

Printed in the United States of America

A mother bird sat on
her egg.

The egg jumped.

"Oh oh!" said the mother bird. "My baby will be here! He will want to eat."

"I must get something
for my baby bird to
eat!" she said. "I will be
back!"

So away she went.

The egg jumped. It
jumped, and jumped, and
jumped!

Out came the baby
bird!

"Where is my mother?"
he said.

He looked for her.

He looked up. He did
not see her.

He looked down. He did
not see her.

"I will go and look for
her," he said.

So away he went.

Down, out of the tree
he went.

16

Down, down, down! It was a long way down.

The baby bird could
not fly.

He could not fly, but
he could walk. "Now I
will go and find my
mother," he said.

He did not know what
his mother looked like. He
went right by her. He did
not see her.

He came to a kitten.
"Are you my mother?"
he said to the kitten.

The kitten just looked
and looked. It did not
say a thing.

The kitten was not his
mother, so he went on.

Then he came to a
hen.

"Are you my mother?"
he said to the hen.

"No," said the hen.

The kitten was not
his mother.

The hen was not
his mother.

So the baby bird went on.

"I have to find my
mother!" he said. "But
where? Where is she?
Where could she be?"

Then he came to a
dog.

"Are you my mother?"
he said to the dog.

"I am not your mother.
I am a dog," said the dog.

The kitten was not
his mother.

The hen was not
his mother.

The dog was not
his mother.

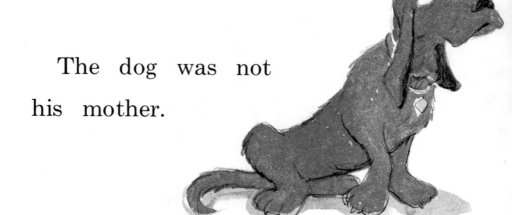

So the baby bird went
on. Now he came to a
cow.

"Are you my mother?"
he said to the cow.

"How could I be your
mother?" said the cow. "I
am a cow."

The kitten and the hen
were not his mother.

The dog and the cow
were not his mother.

Did he have a mother?

"I did have a mother," said the baby bird. "I know I did. I have to find her. I will. I WILL!"

Now the baby bird did
not walk. He ran!

Then he saw a car.
Could that old thing be
his mother? No, it could not.

The baby bird did not
stop. He ran on and on.

Now he looked way,
way down. He saw a
boat. "There she is!" said
the baby bird.

He called to the boat,
but the boat did not
stop.

The boat went on.

He looked way, way up.

He saw a big plane.

"Here I am, Mother,"

he called out.

But the plane did not
stop. The plane went on.

Just then, the baby bird
saw a big thing. This
must be his mother!

"There she is!" he said.
"There is my mother!"

He ran right up to it.
"Mother, Mother! Here
I am, Mother!" he said
to the big thing.

47

But the big thing just
said, "Snort."

"Oh, you are not my
mother," said the baby
bird. "You are a Snort.
I have to get out of
here!"

49

But the baby bird could
not get away. The Snort
went up.

It went way, way up.
And up, up, up went
the baby bird.

51

But now, where was
the Snort going?

"Oh, oh, oh! What is
this Snort going to do to
me? Get me out of here!"

Just then, the Snort
came to a stop.

"Where am I?" said the baby bird. "I want to go home! I want my mother!"

58

Then something
happened.

The Snort put that
baby bird right back in
the tree. The
baby bird was home!

Just then the mother
bird came back to the
tree. "Do you know who
I am?" she said to her
baby.

"Yes, I know who you are," said the baby bird.

"You are not a kitten.

"You are not a hen.

"You are not a dog.

"You are not a cow.

"You are not a boat, or a plane, or a Snort!"

"You are a bird, and you are my mother."